I Told You So!

Strike Three, You're Out!

I Told You So!

Strike Three, You're Out!

Mark Gunning

Itchygooney Books

ISBN 978-0-9950670-4-2

Itchygooney Books
Niagara Falls, Ontario
www.itchygooneybooks.com

Dedicated to: My mom and dad for putting up with all the crazy things I did as a kid. Thanks for letting me be a kid! Also, to all the RUSH fans out there.

Acknowledgments: This book was made with the help of Stephanie Sims, my faithful editor. Also, a big thank you to Ivan and Jeanine R.

Books by Mark Gunning

Available in Print and eBook

I Told You So!
> The Adventures of William and Thomas

I Told You So!
> The Journey Continues

I Told You So!
> Strike Three, You're Out!

Coming

I Told You So!
> Back 4 More!

www.itchygooneybooks.com

www.facebook.com/itchygooneybooks/

Table of Contents

Chapter 1
Return of the Ramp

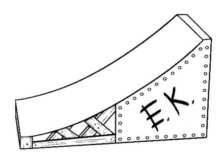

Nearly a month had passed since I last saw or talked to William. No one had seen a sign of William since he fell through the ceiling after trying to pull off a prank on his poor grandma. My mom didn't seem to be fazed by this and seemed more relaxed since William had disappeared. Every time I asked about William, my mom would change the subject. I had a strong feeling that my parents knew exactly where he was, but they didn't want to share this information with me. I had been sending text messages every day in hope that he'd respond. I walked into my room and noticed I had a recent text message waiting for me. Quickly, I grabbed my phone and looked to see who it was from.

Today 9:15 AM

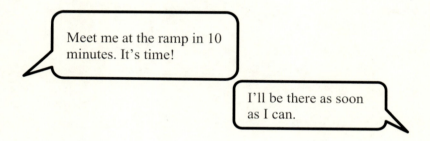

Meet me at the ramp in 10 minutes. It's time!

I'll be there as soon as I can.

I headed to the kitchen to grab a quick bite to eat and then gathered my stuff and headed for William's. I brought my bike as it would be the fastest way there. I wheeled up the driveway and noticed a figure sitting at the top of the ramp. I rode up to the bottom of the ramp and slowly lowered my bike to the ground. I then quickly ran up the ramp and proceeded to sit down beside the figure. Zoey slowly turned her head and smiled. With William disappearing, Zoey and I had been hanging out more often. Over this time period I soon discovered that she wasn't as bad as I had made her out to be. Zoey was actually pretty cool and was in a way, a bit like William. (But a girl!)

William and I had left the ramp still sitting at the end of his driveway (much to the dismay of his mother) and realized that it could still be used for entertainment purposes. Zoey had recently been practicing her jumps and felt very confident that she could beat William's previous record of twelve kids. We had been using a tape measure to record her distance and found that she was jumping just far enough to clear thirteen kids. Zoey felt that she was ready to make the jump later in the day. I agreed with her and we began to plan things out. Since William wasn't around, I decided to create the plans for Zoey myself. She didn't want to have a huge crowd like William did. Instead, she only wanted me to record the event on video so it could be posted directly to YouTube. I grabbed my backpack off my bike and searched quickly for my tablet. Within minutes I had created a set of plans that looked amazing! Just like William, I had made a few plans to make it official. The first plan looked similar to William's plan he had drawn for his historic bike jump. However, this time it showed Zoey flying through the air with tassels streaming from her handlebars, and her long hair flowing in the wind. I included a message with it, pointing out that there were thirteen kids. I knew this would bug William just a tad if he saw it.

In the second part of the plan, it showed Zoey receiving William's old trophy for the longest bike jump. William would be so mad if he knew what we were up to. However, at that moment I didn't care, William had not gotten back to me in over a month.

I showed Zoey the plans and she quickly nodded and smiled. She was happy and ready to attempt the jump. After a brief discussion, Zoey said she would be ready to jump in about two hours. She wanted to head home to make sure she had on the right 'outfit'. I wasn't going to argue with her about that, so I agreed to meet her at the ramp around noon.

She jumped on her bike and headed towards her house. Since I had a few hours to waste, I decided to go home and make sure my camera was ready to record the big moment. As I was heading home on my bike, I thought I saw two small shadows in William's bedroom window. I skidded my bike to a screeching halt and stared towards the window. (Was it William?) Then I noticed that it was just William's little brother Adam and he was waving to me. I quickly waved back and then continued on my way home. I think my mind was starting to play tricks on me. Was I in the sun too long?

As soon as I got home, I ran to my room and gathered my camera, tripod and other items to make sure they were ready. It didn't take me long to test everything. It was all ready to go!

Boredom was starting to set in, so I thought it would be neat to send out a message to everyone telling them that Zoey was about to attempt the jump, but then remembered that she didn't like to get any attention. I quickly changed my mind and waited patiently for the time to pass. It seemed like forever until it was time to go. I grabbed my stuff and raced to meet up with Zoey.

We arrived almost at the same time and I could tell Zoey was getting anxious. She was very quiet, and I knew exactly what to do. I would set up my camera and let her be. It didn't take me very long to set up my equipment, then I went back over to see how Zoey was doing. She told me she was ready, and that she wanted a few practice approaches just to get her confidence up. As she was practicing, I double checked to make sure my camera equipment was ready to go. Everything looked good and Zoey nodded to let me know she was ready. Just in case, I grabbed a tape measure out of my backpack and placed a marker down on the exact spot William landed when he hit the tree branch. All Zoey had to do was go past the marker and the record was hers.

I got into position to video and Zoey headed off

down the driveway and stopped in the same spot William had been when he set the record. I couldn't believe how cool Zoey was and felt quite proud that she had the guts to try and break the record. She then adjusted her helmet and took a test run towards the ramp. Her speed was amazing, and things were looking good. She circled around the ramp and headed back down the driveway and stopped, facing the ramp. I began recording and found a spot that would allow me to get good footage. Zoey steadied her bike and then waved to let me know she was ready. It only took her a second or two and she was on her way. I moved around to the side of the ramp and decided to capture Zoey's jump from the side. She hit the ramp with perfect speed and flew off the end, floating gracefully through the air. As she was about to hit the ground, there was the familiar sound of another bike hitting the ramp. I spun back towards the ramp and couldn't believe my eyes. It was William and he was flying through the air on his bike, with no shirt on. I watched him fly by as Zoey landed and skidded her bike to a halt. William must have hit the ramp with tremendous speed as he landed farther than Zoey and struggled to stop on his landing. Instead of dumping his bike to stop, William kept trying to stay upright. Something must have happened to his brakes. The bad thing about this was there was a small creek running behind his house and William was heading straight for it. I kept recording as I anticipated what was going to happen next. William couldn't stop and he disappeared down the bank and out of view. Almost instantly there was a huge splash and then the sound of William celebrating. William had somehow managed to steal Zoey's thunder. How?

Both Zoey and I stood and stared in disbelief over what had just happened. For a split second, Zoey had beaten William's previous distance he cleared during his record-breaking jump. Only to have it taken away in a blink of an eye.

Then William emerged from the creek and stood at the top of the bank holding his muddied bike over his head. As I looked closer, I noticed that William was covered in blood suckers. He must have hit the bottom of the creek and as he was getting out, they must have latched on. William then shouted, "I am the best!" Then he realized that he was covered with blood suckers and dropped the bike and ran for his house screaming. And just like that, William was back.

Chapter 2
The Pitching Machine

I looked out my window and saw William and his grandfather checking out an old vintage car. The car belonged to William's grandfather, who was a classic car fanatic. His grandpa would bring the car out of storage a couple times a year and enter it in the local Itchygooney Car Show. He always came in second place and was dead set on winning it this year. I decided to go and see what William was up to, and why he had been gone away for so long.

Once I got there it didn't take very long to get the

whole story. Turns out William was sent to a local private school to 'be straightened out', as he called it. His parents had finally had it with his recent antics and his poor grandma was nearing a breakdown. The falling through the ceiling was the last straw for Granny Grunt.

Apparently, William had a three-strikes and you're out policy with the headmaster of the private school. William's dad was a friend of the headmaster and had worked out an agreement with him. However, it only took William a month to reach the 'quota' as he called it. William was kindly asked to pack up his belongings and return home. In a way, I was happy that things didn't work out for William at his new school. Things weren't quite the same without William and his master plans. Don't get me wrong, Zoey was a very cool girl, but she certainly wasn't William.

William's grandpa was getting his car ready for the upcoming show and wanted to make sure it was in tip-top shape. He put William in charge of waxing the car. As soon as William was finished, he said he'd text me to come over and see his latest plans. I ran back home to tell my mom about the great news. However, by the look on her face, she wasn't as thrilled as I was about William being back. It didn't matter. I was excited about his new plans. I decided to go through my collection of baseball and hockey cards to kill some time. Almost an hour later, William texted me to come to his house. I grabbed my gear and headed out the door.

It had only been a month since William and I had been together, but it seemed more like a year. I was so happy that I had a grin from ear to ear as I entered his garage and headed for the workbench. As always, William had a set of plans on the bench ready for me to examine. He was so impressed by my recent plans for the ramp, that he designed his on his computer as well. They were even more awesome than usual!

Plan A

110 to 220 V

Gunner

Awesome Power!

William and I both loved baseball and this time he had a set of plans that I had mentioned to him before summer ended. He actually listened to me for once. Plan A involved a pitching machine that his dad had brought home from the sports store where he worked a few years earlier. In the plan, William was going to increase the power to the machine by hooking up a bigger motor that was running on 220 volts, instead of the usual 110. This would create some awesome power. We had found the motor on an air compressor that someone was throwing out and brought it back to my dad's shop to store for such an occasion. With a bit of work and some modifications, we could swap the motors and create the fastest pitching machine ever. Or at least what we thought would be.

We had always wanted to try and hit a 100 mph fastball, and this was our chance! His dad happened to have a radar gun (again from the sports store) for pitching and we could use it to help set the speed of the machine. Now all we needed to do was gather up the materials and get to work on the modifications. William and I decided it was best to set the machine up at my house as my dad had an outlet with 220 volts and a super long extension cord to go with it. At my house there was a perfect spot where we could set the machine up and attempt to hit the balls without breaking anything.

As soon as we had all the materials, we headed over to my dad's shop to start the modifications.

With a little help from YouTube, we were ready to test out the machine in a couple of hours. It was at this time that William showed me the second part of the plan. It was a plan with William hitting a 100 mph fastball. He even added the word 'slugger' to demonstrate his hitting ability. I wasn't going to argue with him, so I smiled and began to grab the items we would need.

Carefully we set the machine up and put on our batting helmets. We then decided to make a batter's box with some spray paint and hung a large rubber mat off some pipes as our backstop. To be safe, we would adjust the machine by aiming it at the mat. As I adjusted the machine, William pulled out his dad's radar gun and began fidgeting with it.

It was surprisingly easy to set the machine to 100 mph and we were ready to try it. William allowed me to go first as he figured I wouldn't be able to hit the ball anyways. I stepped into the batter's box and got ready. William held up the ball and then placed it in the machine. At the top of the machine there was a tube to place the balls, but he decided to only use one at the start. The first pitch was a blur as I took a huge swing and completely missed it. One by one, William loaded one ball at a time into the machine. After roughly twenty swings without any success, I decided to bunt. I squared up the bat and bunted the ball. It exploded off the bat as my hands

17

stung from the intense vibration. I dropped the bat to the ground and shook my hands. It was William's turn and we gathered up the balls which hadn't gone very far, to my dismay.

As we were doing this, William's grandpa pulled his classic car out of the garage and parked it in the driveway next door. Then he hopped out and headed inside. The sun shone off the freshly waxed paint and the two of us stood and admired the car for a second or two. Then it was back to work. Once all the balls were gathered up, it was William's turn. He stepped into the box and pointed towards Mrs. Bumble's house. He was calling his shot. One by one I loaded a ball into the machine as it made a loud humming sound. To my amazement, William started making contact with the ball immediately. He managed to hit a few grounders, which was more than I could manage. By about the fifteenth pitch, William was making some pretty decent contact. He motioned for me to stop and gathered up the balls.

William then came over and asked me to increase the speed of the machine. He wanted it set at 110 mph. I turned the speed dial a tiny bit and sent a few pitches as he aimed the radar gun. It was perfect. He then decided that he wanted to load the machine with all the balls and go on a rampage as he described it. It was at this moment that I advised him that it was a bad idea. As always, William ignored my warnings and got ready to hit.

The machine had a remote that could be used to send a pitch. He waved to me that he was ready, and I clicked the remote to send the first pitch. As the ball came out, we could hear the machine starting to make some strange sounds. Then it started to shake, and smoke began coming out of the motor. I clicked the remote again to stop the machine, but it had a mind of its own as it started to pick up speed. The machine shook violently and began hurling fastballs towards William's grandpa's car. Thud! Thud! Thud! We both ran for cover!

William's grandpa came running down the driveway and headed for the pitching machine. By the time he managed to pull the cord it was too late. Roughly twenty baseballs had been thrown at his grandpa's car.

It looked like a scene from a horror movie. Except this time the victim was a car. There were numerous dents and a few shattered windows. The two of us grimaced as we stared at his grandpa who stood with his face buried in his hands. I didn't know what else to do so I just turned and walked towards my house. I looked back to see William standing beside his grandpa patting him on the back. This time, there were no words to describe what had just happened. William had finally gone too far. What a shame the car had to suffer such a fate. I went into my room and wondered how long it would be until William got a hold of me.

Chapter 3
Grunt-X

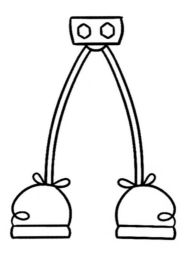

William and I were watching TV when an info-commercial came on for the TRX Suspension Trainer. It didn't take long for William's brain to start working on his next plan. Without saying a word, William jumped up off the couch, did a few burpees, and headed for the garage. I followed him in to watch him go to work. It was amazing how fast he came up with his own version of the TRX.

On his computer, William had drawn a diagram of the trainer and included a well labelled diagram of all the parts he would need. (This diagram would make our teacher proud!) He spun around proudly with the new plan and asked me to help him find the correct supplies. I knew my dad would have most of them, so I took a picture of his plan and we departed for my house. Here's what he had designed.

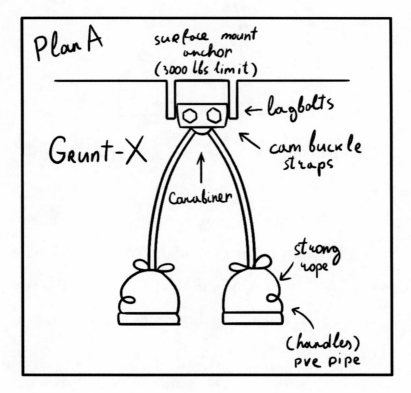

We quickly headed into the backyard and went straight into my dad's shop. I was so excited; I didn't even ask William why he was building one. It didn't take us long to find most of the items. My dad had a large assortment of cam buckle straps and I knew he wouldn't miss them if we took a couple. The same could be said for rope, as my dad had a huge collection of different lengths of high-quality rope. Below his workbench he had many lag bolts and we figured 2.5-inch bolts would do the trick. (Just for extra precaution, we grabbed a handful of 3-inch too!)

William and I then looked very carefully for a carabiner that had a high rating, just in case we needed it to support a lot of weight. (William was going to do the trick!) We were very close to having all the materials. It was now down to the handles and what I felt was the most important part: the surface mount anchor to hold everything in place. My dad had several storage containers that had almost every conceivable hardware item you could think of. Unfortunately, we couldn't find a good enough anchor, so we figured one of us would have to head off to Canadian Tire to buy one. William asked me to take care of the handles while he ran home to beg his grandma to drive him to the store. We agreed on an approximate time and he took off for home.

I knew exactly where to look. My dad collected any PVC piping that his friends were throwing out and stored it in the rafters on the second floor of his shop. I couldn't believe all the different sized pipes he had. After a few minutes of testing the diameter of the pipes in my hand, I found one that felt just right for the handles. I pulled a length of it down from the ceiling and brought it downstairs to cut. I made it roughly four fingers wider than my hand and made the cut. It was easy to cut through with a hacksaw, and I was finished in minutes. Since I had some time to waste, I cleaned up the mess we had made and packed up all the items into my backpack for later. I then hustled to my house so I could grab a quick bite to eat and then head back to William's. Before I was to head over, I had to wait for William to text me. Once the text arrived, I was on my way.

We quickly met in the garage and William showed me the bracket he got at Canadian Tire. The guy working there assured William that the bracket would not break or come out of the floor joist if we used the proper lag bolts. (Remember, I was always concerned about safety!)

Just to be on the safe side, William and I went on the Internet and researched how to tie the handles properly. After viewing a few different versions, we settled on the fact that most of the videos recommended using a bowline knot. It took a bit of practice, but we soon had the handles tied up to the cam straps and were ready to head to his basement to attach it to the floor joist in the furnace room. Quickly, we gathered up all the materials and were ready to go.

When we got downstairs, there was a huge mess in the furnace room. William's dad was putting in a laminate floor in another area and had brought his prized possessions and stacked them next to the furnace. The collection of boxes contained his dad's hockey and baseball cards that he had collected since he was a kid. He had many of the rookie cards signed and William and I were only allowed to see them if his dad was around and was holding them. His dad was so paranoid that he usually had them locked up. Unfortunately, he must have moved them from his office temporarily to do the flooring job. Since his dad was away, William decided that it would be okay if we just moved the boxes and set them out of the way. I didn't really see it being a problem, so I agreed with him and we carefully started to move the boxes. It took us about five minutes to get the cards moved and we were back on our way to hanging the TRX system. William decided to give it a better name and settled on calling it the Grunt-X Trainer. He chose this because his grandma had kindly taken him to the store to get the hardware to hang it.

William stood and stared at the ceiling for a bit and then chose a spot that was above the hot water heater. Directly above the tank were two floor joists that would be perfect for securing the anchor. Between the two joists was a 2 x 4 that had a water line running through it. I thought it would be best to attach to either face of the beams. William thought it would be easier to attach the anchor to the bottom of the cross piece. I encouraged him to think carefully about his location. After a moment, he settled on attaching directly to the bottom of the piece with the water line. It was easier to drill a pilot hole straight up to screw the bolts in, than to try and use the drill between the joists and attach it to the bracket on the side. I had a bad feeling about the placement, but William assured me that this wouldn't be a problem. He then pulled out the second part of the plan and carefully stuck it to the wall. It was a picture of William and what William thought he would look like after using the workout apparatus. He had drawn himself with huge arms! I laughed for a second or two and then prepared myself for our next task.

We headed off to get a ladder and a few tools to help secure the bracket. It only took a few minutes for us to have the Grunt-X in place. William decided to be nice and let me try it out first. We adjusted the straps and I tried a few pull ups with it. Then I attempted to do a front push-up. It was a lot harder than it looked on TV and I failed miserably. William gave me his disappointed look and then attempted it himself. Amazingly, he was able to do a few front push-ups before tiring. We both figured it would get easier the more we did it. I figured we were done with it for the day when William decided to aim his back at the ground and pull himself up. It looked cool as he did some reverse pulls. William finished and then stood up. He stared at it for a moment and then said we needed to test it for strength. According to him, it would be strong enough to hold the two of us. Now I was worried.

We both grabbed onto one handle each and began the weight test. It appeared that William was right. The bracket was holding our weight with no problem. However, William wasn't quite satisfied yet. He suggested that as we were hanging, we could tug as hard as we could to prove the bracket was strong enough. I was a little hesitant, but thought, what could go wrong. So, we grabbed the handles and with all the force we could muster, pulled on the handles as hard as we could. That's when things went horribly wrong!

Remember when William decided to use the cross piece instead of the actual floor joist to hold the bracket? Well, the cross piece wasn't strong enough and it basically broke in half. As the two of us came slamming to the floor, the main water line coming towards the hot water tank split wide open. It began spraying water all over the furnace room and surrounding area. William reacted calmly and walked over to the main shutoff valve and started trying to turn it off. Unfortunately, the tap was seized, and he couldn't budge it. Thinking quickly,

I grabbed a pair of pliers from a table and handed them to William. He clamped them onto the handle and gave them a mighty twist. Instead of turning the water off, he broke the tap handle completely off. (The Grunt-X must have been working!) By now almost everything that was nearby was soaked. It was at this point that we both noticed his dad's collection of sports cards. We began screaming for his grandma to come and help.

Granny Grunt came hustling down the stairs and screamed. Then we pointed at the water and the soaking wet boxes. I didn't think it was possible, but his grandma had another level of hollering that we'd never heard before. Once she had finished her outburst, she headed upstairs to call a plumber. As this was going on, we grabbed the boxes and moved them to another location in the basement. It wasn't looking too good.

Surprisingly, the plumber arrived quickly and had the water shut off in less than a minute.

However, the damage had been done. For the next three hours, William and I began carrying the soaked boxes to the garage where they could be examined. His dad's cards took the worst of the flood and William knew his dad would be devastated. I could tell he was truly sorry for what had happened. During all the moving of the boxes, William hardly said a word. Once we had all the boxes moved, we went back down to start mopping up the water. It took us another three hours to finish. As I was about to head up the stairs to go home for the evening, I noticed the bracket was still screwed to the 2 x 4 that was lying on the floor. I caught William's attention and showed him the bracket and told him he was right. It was strong enough. William then stared at me, pointed towards the top of the stairs and turned around. I took this action as he wasn't too happy with my comment. I quickly headed up the stairs and went home for the night.

A few days passed when William texted to tell me what had happened when his dad got home. His dad was extremely upset as we figured he'd be. However, an insurance agent came by and assessed the damage. Luckily, they were going to cover the damage and his dad was going to be receiving a cheque to cover the cost of his cards. The good thing was his dad had carefully made a list of all the cards he had and what the value of them were worth. The downside for William, he was going to have to spend the next few weeks working with his dad to redo the basement and search the Internet to find replacement cards for the ones he had damaged during the workout gone wrong.

As for the Grunt-X invention, William's dad moved it to a better location and tested it himself to make sure it was safe. Hey, even his dad thought it was a cool idea.

Chapter 4
The Mummy

It was the day before Halloween and William was ready for his next great plan. He was so pumped when the day finally arrived for him to share his plan with me because he had been planning it for almost two months. Every year William got super excited at Halloween time. He was always trying to scare the teacher or principal by pulling some type of prank. I was hoping this was the year that he would pull off the master of all plans.

We were sitting in class when he passed me a copy of his latest plan. I studied it very carefully. On the page was an illustration of William wearing a scary mummy costume. It looked so cool. I passed it back to him but unfortunately got the attention of Mr. Mousseau. Our teacher didn't like us passing notes, but rather enjoyed the fact that it kept William and I quiet in the classroom. Instead he gave us the look and went right back to teaching a

math lesson to the class. I quietly whispered to William to tell me more about the plan at first break.

The bell rang and William was the first one out the door. I quickly met up with him at his locker and asked for a few details. However, since we had to go eat in the classroom, he wasn't too keen on sharing his ideas until we were outside. He didn't want anyone to hear and spoil the surprise.

It seemed like forever waiting for the bell to go. Finally, it rang, and we headed to our lockers to drop off our lunch pails and head outside. Once we were done, we headed straight for a quiet spot where we would be left alone to discuss the plans. William reached into his pocket and pulled out the plan from earlier. He then went on to explain what was going on. Since it was Halloween the next day, William was going to dress up like a mummy and scare the entire school during the end of the month assembly. Every year our principal Mr. Pitts would invite all the classes down to the gym in the morning. He would then turn the lights down low and tell the school a scary story. Unfortunately, for us, the stories were toned down so the kindergarten kids wouldn't be frightened too much. I guess that was a good idea on his part.

This year William planned to dress up like a mummy and hide behind the stage. Then, when the lights went out, he would rush to the centre of the stage and moan as loud as he could just before the

lights started to come back on. The plan was to scare the entire school, and especially our principal.

My job at all school functions was to run the lights. (Likely a plan of Mr. Pitts to keep me out of trouble.) Since I was running the lights, I would be able to turn them on at the best moment. William explained to me that he would ask to go to the bathroom right at the start of the assembly so he could sneak backstage and get wrapped up in his mummy costume. He then proceeded to show me the second part of his plan. It was a plan of him moaning and scaring the entire school. This looked like it was going to be an awesome prank! The bell rang to line up and the two of us ran to get ready.

For the rest of the day, we giggled every time we looked at each other. It got so bad at one point, that Mr. Mousseau finally told William to leave and go read in the hall. It seemed like forever, but the school day finally ended, and we packed up and headed home on the bus. William wanted me to come over to his house right away to help him make his costume.

It didn't take us long to get it ready. He decided to use what he thought was one of his old bed sheets for the cloth. My job was to help cut it into strips. It was at this point that I mentioned it looked like a rather expensive sheet. I was quickly assured by William that it was old, and his mom wouldn't miss it. To solve the problem of it looking too clean, William took it outside and began to rub it on the ground. After about thirty minutes, he had it looking like old Egyptian cotton. We headed back inside to cut it into strips. It didn't take us long to find a few different mummy costume ideas on Google before finding one that explained the right way to wrap it up. With a bit of practice, we had it perfected. It was getting close to suppertime, so I decided to head home for the night.

The next morning William and I met up at the bus stop. Other kids had their costumes with them as well, so no one bothered to ask William what he had in his bag. Things were going just as planned. The bus arrived at school and we headed to the back of the school. It wouldn't be long, and the mummy would be unleashed!

The bell rang and we headed into the school and put our belongings in our lockers. I could tell right away William was getting a bit too excited about the whole thing. Within minutes, we were led down the hallway and into our classroom by our teacher Mr. Mousseau. It was obvious by the look on his face that Halloween day at school wasn't his favourite day. After a few minutes, we settled in and sang the anthem, listened to a bunch of announcements, and then started reading quietly to ourselves.

The PA came back on shortly and asked all the classes in the school to come down to the gym, starting with the oldest grades first. Slowly, we all made our way to the gym and I got positioned on a chair by the light switch. I gave Mr. Pitts a big thumbs up to show him I was ready. I spotted William sitting nearby with our class. He had an enormous smile on his face. As the assembly went on, William asked our teacher if he could go to the bathroom. He jumped up and headed out the door. I couldn't wait for William to appear from nowhere on the stage and frighten the entire school.

The strange thing was, that for October 31st, it was extremely hot outside. The weather was unusually warm at this time of the year. William must have been too hot and for that reason, things took a turn for the worse, I'd say. However, I'll tell you more about this as I tell the rest of the story. The principal headed to the front of the stage on the floor and motioned for me to turn off most of the gym lights. As I was about to turn them off, I noticed William out of the corner of my eye heading up the stairs towards the stage in his mummy costume. He looked just like a real live mummy, or should I say a dead one?

As the story was being told, William carefully made his way to the centre of the stage in the dark. Our principal was using a small flashlight to keep his face lit to make it seem even scarier. When Mr. Pitts paused for a moment, William let out a piercing shriek. I immediately turned the lights on and there was William standing only in his underwear right in front of the entire school. The little kids screamed, the teachers gasped, and the intermediate kids broke out into laughter. William quickly tried to cover himself and ran off the stage. Once the entire school had calmed down, we were all sent back to our rooms. Poor William was sent to the office. His mom was called to come pick him up.

Later that night, William texted me to explain what had happened. As he was fumbling his way to the stage in the dark, he caught his wrap on something sharp and his costume began to unravel. Since it was so hot, he had decided to strip down to just his underwear to stay cool. That explained why he was only wearing underwear when the lights came on. In a panic, he had no idea what to do and screamed when it happened. That's when I turned on the lights thinking it was his signal to scare everyone. From that day on, it was known as the best Halloween day at my school ever!

Chapter 5
Whoopee

A few weeks had gone by when William decided it was time for his next prank. The Halloween ordeal had slowed him down just a bit. (The good thing about William was nothing actually slowed him down.) He was maintaining a low profile when he found an ad for a Whoopee cushion in one of his dad's old comic books. I received a short text requesting my presence at his house within the next half hour.

William

Today 9:15 AM

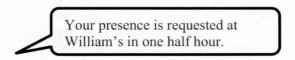

Your presence is requested at
William's in one half hour.

I quickly grabbed some of my belongings and
threw them into my backpack. Within minutes, I
was standing in his garage staring at his latest set of
plans. The first plan showed William placing a
Whoopee cushion on Mr. Mousseau's chair.

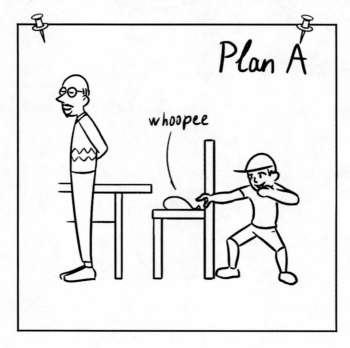

I was already interested in this plan as soon as I saw the word 'whoopee'.

My job was to help him find a Whoopee cushion. That's when I pulled out my laptop and started searching Amazon for the best deal. Within minutes, we had found several options. Surprisingly, there were a lot of different options to choose from. There were bright coloured ones. Giant ones to wear as costumes and even poop shaped ones. However, William was a bit old-school and decided to get the classic pink one. We found one that came in a set with five other pranks called Pranks in a Tin. He figured that he would have other uses for the rest of the set and could hang on to them for the right occasion. The cool thing was William's mom had an Amazon Prime membership and we could use it to get super fast shipping for free. It only took a few minutes and we had ordered the set to arrive in a couple days. Now all we had to do was wait.

A few days later, William jumped off the bus and headed straight for his house. I ran behind him and had a hard time keeping up with him. Sitting on his front porch was a box from Amazon. It had arrived! Without saying a word, he picked it up and ran into his house. I followed him inside and headed upstairs to his room. On the way in, his mom tried to say hello. I managed to give a quick wave as I flew up the stairs.

William tore the box open and grabbed the prank box. He then held it up in front of him waiting for me to take a picture. I snapped a few shots as he was tearing off the wrapping. The contents of the box were quickly dumped onto his desk. Sitting on the desk was a collection of some classic pranks. Both of us smiled as he picked up the Whoopee cushion and began squeezing it. The two of us laughed as it blurted out various farting sounds. For the next twenty minutes, we busted our guts as we took turns sitting on it. Eventually, his mom came upstairs to see what was going on. She popped her head in the door and saw us rolling on the floor in tears. She looked at the items on the table, shook her head, and walked away. It was time for us to find our first victim. William called for his little brother Adam to come to his room.

Adam arrived almost instantly to see what William had wanted and was told to stand by William's chair and to close his eyes. Adam hesitated for a second and then closed them. William slipped the cushion on the chair and then asked Adam to sit down. His brother slowly sat down which made the sounds come out a little bit slower than normal. A look of shock came across Adam's face as he wasn't prepared for the surprise. All three of us laughed at the sounds it made. We played with it for a bit longer and then decided it was time for a break. William threw it back on his desk and then pulled out the long awaited second part of his plan. It was our teacher Mr. Mousseau, sitting on a Whoopee cushion with the entire class laughing at him.

I loved how William tried to write the sounds of what the cushion would make. The plan was to go into action sometime tomorrow at school. I was to cause a distraction while William snuck it on his chair. Once we went over the plans, William tossed them on his desk, and we went outside to play catch. Eventually, my mom called for me for dinner and I headed home. The big day would have to wait until tomorrow.

The next day, William and I arrived at school and he carefully showed me the contents of his backpack. Hidden in a side compartment was the cushion. Minutes later the bell rang, and we entered the school. Now all we had to do was wait for the perfect opportunity. William thought the best time to pull off the prank was to do the trick after the first break. The class would be reading silently and that would make for the best time to, shall I say, have a blast!

First break ended and we came into the class and followed the routine of getting a book to read quietly. William had brought the cushion into the class under his shirt and hid it in his desk. It was no surprise that his desk was right near the teacher's desk. The whole class was reading silently when we both noticed Mr. Mousseau fidgeting with his computer. It appeared there was something wrong with it. He looked to place it down on his desk, but it was piled with too much stuff, so he carefully set it on the floor beside his chair and stood to look for something in his cupboard. That's when William jumped up and placed the Whoopee cushion on his chair without being noticed. Now all we had to do was wait for our teacher to sit down!

It only took Mr. Mousseau a minute to find a power cord for his computer. Without looking down, he spun his chair around and plopped down on the seat. The next few minutes were awesome! The class was subjected to a series of sounds.

The first thing we all heard was a loud **"Brrraaapp!!!!!!"** Heads spun to see what was going on. The entire class was jolted away from reading by an enormous farting sound. The second sound was Mr. Mousseau shouting out, "OH MY!" But guess what? That wasn't it. All this was followed by a sizzling sound. Then the familiar sound of our teacher's voice. "William!!!"

I bet you're all wondering what happened. Right? Well, it turns out that William's little brother Adam must have filled the Whoopee cushion with some water the night before. William, without realizing, placed the cushion on the chair with the tail of the cushion facing out. As Mr. Mousseau spun the chair, it had stopped facing the direction of his laptop on the floor. As he quickly sat down the force of the impact squeezed the water out of the cushion and sent it directly onto the keyboard and screen of the laptop. The sizzling sound was the computer being fried. Then the laptop began puffing out smoke. Mr. Mousseau had the class leave the classroom until he felt it was safe to go back in. Without even saying a word or being told to, William headed straight for the office.

To make up for accidentally destroying our teacher's laptop, William was asked to sell chocolate bars as a fundraiser to replace the laptop. He managed to sell quite a lot of boxes and raised a lot of money for the school. He did so well that he brought in enough money to pay for two brand new computers in our classroom. In a way, the accident was sort of a good thing.

Chapter 6
The Balloon Chair

It was after supper and I was taking shots at my garage door when I noticed William on his front lawn. It appeared that he had some balloons tied to something, but I couldn't tell what it was. So, I dropped my hockey stick, grabbed my bike, and rode over to check things out. As I rode up to William, I noticed a laundry basket sitting on the ground with a bunch of giant balloons tied to it. They must have had helium in them because they were all floating upwards. He smiled and tossed me a crumpled piece of paper. Glancing at the plan, I quickly realized what he was up to. It was a plan with a whole bunch of balloons tied to a laundry basket. Inside the basket were some of his little brother's favourite action figures. (Likely his best ones, I might add.) William was going to try and get the laundry basket to float in the air.

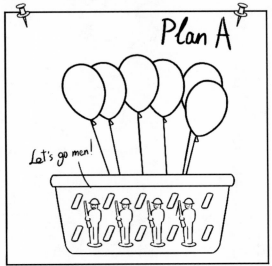

I was curious as to what he had planned this time. It was so interesting, I asked him for more details. It didn't take him long to start explaining everything to me. Apparently, the old record in our neighbourhood for floating objects in the sky was set by using an old shoebox with an egg inside. Dylan had managed to get the box to sail an amazing twenty metres before it got stuck in a nearby tree. William figured he would outdo that record by sending a laundry basket fifty metres in the air with a basket full of GI Joe dolls. (Or should I say, "action figures," as William called them.)

I was wondering where William got all the giant balloons when he told me his dad had brought them home from work after a big sale at the sports store. He also brought home a large cylinder full of helium. It seemed like a reasonable plan to me.

The only problem was that the basket needed some more balloons to get it airborne. We both ran into the garage and filled up some more balloons. Quickly, we ran back to the front lawn and tied the balloons to the basket. William had a weight in the bottom of the basket to keep it from floating away. Without saying a word, he picked up the weight from the basket and the basket started to lift off into the air. It was so cool watching it go up. I didn't think it would work.

The basket with the dolls, (um, I mean action figures) floated up and began heading towards his grandparents' large tree in their front yard. Within minutes, the basket was stuck at the top of the tree. It hadn't made it the fifty metres he was hoping. The two of us laughed. Then I asked him how he would get his brother's toys back down. William wasn't quite sure about that. He smiled and said he'd figure that out later.

Instead of worrying, he looked at me with a twinkle in his eye and ran for the garage and headed for the workbench. I followed him in and sat on a chair as he began to work on another plan on his tablet. It didn't take very long for him to unveil his latest plan. I stared at the screen as William showed me his latest and greatest idea. The plan had a picture of a lawn chair with a ton of balloons. Sitting on the chair was William, and he was chilling. I loved the way he expressed himself in the plan.

It looked cool and dangerous at the same time. (As did most of William's stunts.) I quickly told William how I thought it wasn't such a great idea.

Of course, he ignored my warnings (as he did so most of the time) and began filling more balloons. I was then given a job to start cutting some fishing line to tie to the balloons. Upon further inspection, the line appeared to be fifty-pound test, so it would do the trick if we used enough balloons. As I began tying the line to the balloons, William went back to the table and started writing a list of items he would require for his historic launch.

The awesome thing about William was that he liked to be prepared just in case something bad happened. (Which was most of the time!) I was super curious as to what he thought he would need for his latest adventure. What possibly would he need this time? All the items quickly raced through my mind as I wondered what he needed. Would they be emergency items or just silly things he thought he should take?

It didn't take long and he had a list ready to go. I looked it over quickly to see just what he thought he needed. Now all we had to do was locate all the items on the list.

Here is what he wanted:

```
┌─────────────────────────────────────────────┐
│                                               │
│         Balloon Chair Supplies                │
│                                               │
│    1)   Helmet (protect coconut)              │
│    2)   Camera (cool shots)                   │
│    3)   Food (might need it)                  │
│    4)   Slingshot (way to get back down)      │
│    5)   Passport (you just never know)        │
│    6)   Flashlight (tactical light)           │
│    7)   Water (need to stay hydrated)         │
│    8)   Pee Bottle (see number 7)             │
│    9)   Cell Phone (to call for help, yeah right!) │
│    10)  Life jacket (near the water)          │
│    11)  Lightsaber (Use the force Luke!)      │
│                                               │
└─────────────────────────────────────────────┘
```

It didn't take us long to gather all the items and have them packed up for him. Being a nice guy, I emptied my backpack and put all the items into it for William. Once this was done, we continued to fill the rest of the balloons and prepare them to be attached to the chair. I was so excited as I thought this was one of the coolest ideas William had ever thought up.

Roughly an hour had passed as we continued to attach the balloons to the chair. As we added more and more balloons, the chair began to float into the air. We quickly took care of the problem by tying the legs of the chair to an old fence post that was sticking out of the ground in his yard. This made it easier for us to focus on the tying of the balloons. William explained that the most important part of the setup was making sure we had each balloon attached securely. I couldn't agree more.

Eventually, we had all the balloons attached and the chair was ready for lift-off. William then went over the safety plans he had prepared earlier. I would be on the ground holding onto a support line that would keep William from floating away. To make sure he didn't float away, I'd have to reel him back down once he gave the signal. At roughly the thirty-metre mark, he would take some aerial shots from above. My job was to shoot a video from the ground. This video would be proof of his amazing stunt. It was to then be uploaded to YouTube for millions to see and enjoy.

We decided to use some nylon rope that my dad had lying around for the safety line. We used a tape measure and put a mark at the thirty-metre point on the line. Once this was done, I used clinch knots to secure the rope to the chair and the old fence post. I quickly noticed that the post was rotted quite a bit where it came out of the ground and told William, but he blew off my comment and proceeded on. William checked over his supplies carefully and put on his helmet. The big moment had arrived!

William positioned himself into the chair and then used a ratcheting tie down strap to secure himself to the chair. This was done as a safety precaution. As you know, William took safety quite seriously. I handed him the backpack and checked my cell phone to make sure I was ready to record. I was very excited and could hardly wait for William to float off. He did a quick inventory of the items in the backpack and gave me a thumbs up signal. He was ready to go.

Just as William was hopefully about to add his name to the neighbourhood list of records, Zoey and Adam came from around the garage and ran to see what was going on. I filled them in on everything and then asked Zoey to record William as I watched the rope. I asked them to step back so I could prepare for launch.

For a bit of added drama, I decided to start my countdown with T-10 (T minus ten). I knew Adam would get a kick out of this. T-10, nine, eight, seven, six, five, four, three, two, one. BLAST OFF!!! I cut the lines holding the chair to the post and we watched William float up into the sky. It was actually working! He floated up and up until I saw that the thirty-metre mark was coming up on the line. As it hit the mark, I grabbed the rope and stopped William from going any higher. William pulled out his camera and started taking photos from above. The three of us stood and admired William in all his glory. He took off his helmet and waved it in his hand for a few seconds and then scrambled to put it back on.

It appeared to me that he was showing off at this point. Zoey smiled and mentioned how brave William was. I believe that's the point where I mumbled something like more stupid than brave. Zoey asked me what I said but I just smiled. As all of this was going on, a breeze came in and began pushing William towards the river that ran in front of our houses. The breeze began to get stronger and stronger. The tension on the rope was increasing. It was likely a good time to start bringing him back down. Then the weirdest thing happened. William started swinging his arms in circles and pointed up. Was this his signal to come down? The one thing we forgot to mention was his signal to come down. It appeared that he wanted to go higher. Adam laughed and jumped up and down. I looked at Zoey and she motioned for me to let out more rope. I hesitantly let out more rope.

William must have been forty metres when he began swinging his arms again. I decided to let out more rope. That's when the breeze really picked up and started blowing. The chair heaved upwards and took William surging higher. The rope was now burning my hands as I tried to slow him down. Zoey grabbed the line and we both started pulling on it. The wind was getting stronger and stronger. We both noticed that the end of the rope was approaching. Something had to be done. The burning was too much and the two of us let go of the rope. William jolted upwards and then there was a loud snapping sound. The three of us screamed in horror.

Amazingly, the rope hadn't broken. William was now roughly fifty metres in the air. He was no longer waving his arms. Instead, it appeared he was holding on to the chair for dear life. I told Adam to run and get his mom. Next, I told Zoey to run to the garage and grab a couple pairs of gloves and hurry back.

As soon as she returned, we put on the gloves and began pulling William back down. By now the wind was super strong and it was giving us quite the workout. William's mom arrived and started pulling on the rope as well. Things were going quite well considering all the circumstances. We had William hauled in about halfway when things went south. Apparently, the line couldn't withstand all the pressure and in a split second, it snapped! The four of us stared helplessly as William floated out towards the river. William's poor mom went hysterical. Zoey tried to comfort her as Adam burst out laughing. I didn't know whether to laugh or cry. We all became silent for a moment when my phone beeped. William was texting me.

Today 7:13 PM

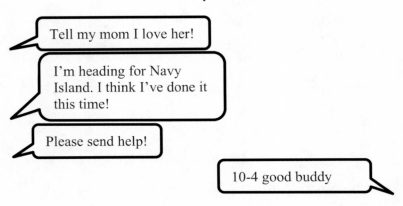

I handed my phone to his mother and she began reading them. She sent a few messages back and then she got on the phone and called for help. It didn't take very long as we could hear sirens off in the distance. They were on their way! As the sirens got louder, William kept texting. He appeared to be in some type of danger.

> I've cleared the water below. Afraid I'm heading towards the States now.

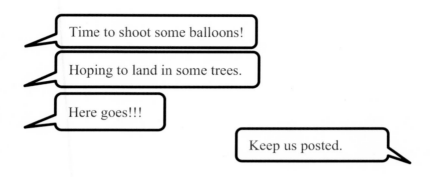

William's mom got in the car and told us all to jump in. Quickly, we headed down the road to the local boat launch to meet the rescuers. We arrived just before they did and got out of the car and watched as the police, fire, and ambulance teams arrived. Paramedic Mike was one of the first ones to approach us and recognized us immediately. After briefly explaining what had happened to William, a crew assembled on the dock as a rescue boat was unloaded from the trailer. One by one, a team of respondents jumped in the boat and headed off towards the island. William's mom and Adam were both visually upset by now and were escorted to the ambulance to relax. Zoey and I stood by the shore and continued to watch.

By now, a rather large crowd of neighbours and bystanders had gathered around the boat launch to see what all the commotion was about. Surprisingly, when they found out what was going on, many of them were not at all shocked. The crowd grew larger and larger as time passed. Then, I received another text from William.

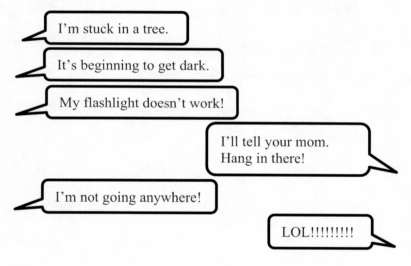

I ran over to tell William's mom that he was okay and that he was stuck in a tree on Navy Island. One of the firefighters checked in to see what was happening and relayed the news to the rescue team.

We could hear calls going back and forth between the rescue team when we were told the news. It was getting too dark and they were having a hard time finding him. They were going to call in a helicopter to help with the search. The leader of the team at the dock asked me to call William on my cell phone. I called and handed it to him. He immediately put it on speaker phone. We could hear the whole conversation going on, when William said he had a plan and hung up. What was he going to do?

It didn't take long for the search and rescue copter to fly by and head for the island. From our vantage point we could see the helicopter flying back and forth over the trees with its spotlight on. Then the message came in that everyone was waiting for. They found him! William was okay and only had a small scratch on his arm.

It took roughly fifteen more minutes, but William was in the boat and heading back to safety. We were all relieved and the crowd began to disperse. A few remained behind to see William arrive and cheered as he climbed out of the boat and onto the dock. One person was even heard saying it was the Bustin Jieber kid again. William rushed to his mom and gave her a big hug. He then turned to me and smiled holding his lightsaber in his hand. Zoey ran over and gave William a big hug as well. Just then Paramedic Mike came over and told William he was a very lucky boy and patted him on the back. Then the rescue team began packing up to go home. Hopefully, this would be the only time we would ever have to rely on them.

A local news reporter from the Itchygooney Times had arrived and stopped William and interviewed him for a bit. William had several photos taken and was finally allowed to head home. Would he become famous? Maybe.

So, I bet you're wondering what happened to William? Right? Once we got back to William's house, he explained everything to all of us over the next hour. It basically went like this. William noticed that he was heading for the States, so he used his slingshot to pop some of the balloons to lose altitude so he wouldn't overshoot the island. Eventually, he came down and landed at the top of one of the big trees on the island. Realizing he was too far up, he texted us to say he was in the tree and it was getting dark. He pulled out his flashlight, but then discovered that it didn't work. He remembered taking the batteries out for one of his other pranks and never replaced them. He then heard the helicopter coming and had another plan. He pulled out his lightsaber and started waving it in the air. It must have worked as the helicopter crew spotted him and airlifted him out of the tree. He was then lowered down to the shoreline. (Which he claims was AWESOME!) From there he was taken back to the mainland by the rescue boat. The force had saved him!

Unfortunately, William's dad was away on

business and missed all the excitement. Maybe it was a good thing for William. As part of his punishment, William was to go to the local fire station and help wash the firetrucks and rescue boat on weekends. He was also banned from using balloons and helium for one year. However, we all agreed on how lucky he really was.

On a positive note for William, a few weeks later, the video of him floating away went viral. He had over a million views in the first few weeks. And once again, William had managed to become a celebrity.

Chapter 7
Rock Stars

We were on our way home on the bus from school when William noticed a pile of junk by Dylan's house. Immediately, he pointed towards it and smiled. Right then I knew he had spotted something good. Likely part of his next great idea. But what?

As soon as the bus pulled up to our stop, William

jumped out of his seat, exited the bus, and headed straight for home. I yelled that I was heading home first and would be right back. I told my mom I was home and was going to go to William's for a bit. She cringed for a moment and then went back to whatever she was doing. I headed over to William's as fast as I could. By the time I got there, William already had his dad's tractor and mini trailer hooked up and was ready to roll. I threw on one of his bike helmets and hopped in the back of the trailer.

The nice thing about the ride was that it was only a few minutes down the road. We arrived at the side of the road to discover that we had hit the jackpot. Dylan's parents must have been cleaning out their garage and finally decided it was time to get rid of Dylan's collection of musical equipment. Years before, Dylan had formed a rock band in his garage. Overnight they made up a song that was simply awesome. Kids from all around came to see them play. The members of the band became superstars at school. Everywhere they went, people knew who they were. Everyone wanted to be just like them. Then the worst thing that you could imagine happened. The band broke up, and just like that, they disappeared overnight. Dylan never talked to anyone about what had happened. Enough on that. Let's get back to the story.

As we headed down the road, William began to explain why we were heading to pick up some trash at the side of the road. As the bus was going by Dylan's house, William noticed a collection of old guitars and amps. We had gone by so fast that he didn't have enough time to process everything he saw from the bus window. We would have to go there and see for ourselves.

Within minutes we pulled up and stopped right beside the pile of junk. It was rock and roll heaven! At first, we thought it must have been a mistake and that someone was coming by to pick up the items.

That thought was quickly put aside as we both noticed the sign that read 'Free Stuff. Please take!!!'

William was off the tractor and grabbing equipment even before I had a chance to get out of the trailer. The first thing he grabbed was a guitar. It was a bit beaten up but had the rock star look to it. Carefully, he placed it in the trailer and began getting other things. There was a bass guitar with a strap and even a couple of old amps. However, the best thing that I noticed was a beat-up set of drums. I had always wanted to be a drummer. It now looked like my dream was about to come true.

Piece by piece we loaded up as much of the equipment as we could and headed back to his house with it. As we were travelling down the road, Zoey noticed us and followed behind on her bike as we made our way. Upon arrival, William pulled up to his garage and hopped off to go open the door. Once the garage door was up, all three of us began unloading the equipment. Then the strangest thing happened. Zoey picked up the old bass guitar that we had brought back, plugged it in, and started playing a song. Amazingly, she was really good at it! It didn't take us long to realize that Zoey must have known how to play. After a few minutes of interrogation, it turned out that her older brother was a former member of Dylan's band and had taught her how to play. That's when William ran to his computer and started creating his next plan. I continued to unload the drums as Zoey helped me. Once we had everything off the wagon, we headed to the bench to see what William was working on.

Of course, William was once again the main centre of attention. He was playing guitar beside an amp and wrote the words 'Future Rock Star!' However, there seemed to be one small problem with his new plan. William didn't know how to play. He turned to Zoey, who was rocking out again and begged her to teach him how to play. She agreed that she would start to teach him the next day.

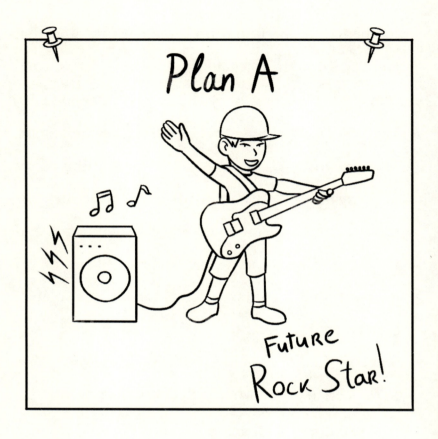

Plan A

FutuRe
RocK StaR!

So, we got permission to set everything up in his garage and planned to meet the next day. I hurried home so I could look up how to play drums on YouTube. As soon as I entered my front door, I greeted my mom with the fantastic news. I had finally decided on the instrument that I wanted to play. It was the drums. The look on my mom's face was priceless. I was pretty sure that she was just as happy as I was. Quickly, I disappeared into my room to start my next journey. The wonderful journey of drums!

It didn't take long for me to find some videos for beginners. I grabbed the drumsticks from my Rock Band set and began pounding on the top of my desk. Just as I was really getting into it, a text message arrived. It was William and he was making sure I was going to come over the next day.

You're coming tomorrow, right?

You bet! I'm practicing right now!

Rock on!

I told my mom I want drum lessons!

Sweet! See you tomorrow.

I put my phone down and got back to playing the drums on my desk. I couldn't wait for the next day to arrive. (My mom too!)

As soon as I woke up, I got dressed and grabbed my drumsticks. It was Saturday morning and we would have the entire weekend to jam! Zoey was already there by the time I got there. She was in the middle of teaching William some power chords when I plopped myself down at the drums and began to play. The two of them both stopped and stared. Either they were shocked at the fact that I was playing something that sounded okay, or I was just so loud that I startled them. (It must have been because I was so good.) Either way, I had their attention.

We spent the entire weekend jamming out and learning how to play. We hardly took any breaks and I think William's mom was surprised as she would pop her head into the garage and ask us every now and then if we were going to take a break. It was so nice she was so concerned about us. We'd just wave at her and continue playing. Time flew and the weekend was coming to an end. We all decided that we would try to practice at least every night if we could for an hour after school. After agreeing to this, we all shook hands to make it official and then headed off. I ran home to share the fantastic news with my parents. It happened to be suppertime when I arrived, so I gulped down my food and headed to my room to practice some more.

The next day at school we all met in the hallway to discuss the important things. No, not school stuff, band stuff. Then like fate would have it, our teacher Mr. Mousseau put up a poster in the hallway. People gathered around and it created quite a stir. Carefully we worked our way to the front of the crowd and stared in awe. It was the greatest thing to happen in our school. Everyone gathered around to see what it was. There right in front of our eyes was a poster for the entire school to see. It was hard to believe!

```
┌─────────────────────────────────────────────┐
│                                               │
│      Itchygooney Public School Presents       │
│                                               │
│           TALENT SHOW                         │
│                                               │
│                                               │
│          Friday October 13th                  │
│          1:00 PM to 3:00 PM                    │
│          Itchygooney Gymnasium                 │
│                                               │
│                                               │
│       Here's your chance to shine!            │
│       Sign up to audition!!!                  │
│                                               │
│                                               │
└─────────────────────────────────────────────┘
```

It was our destiny! We were going to form a band and rock the place out. It was going to be EPIC! The excitement in the school was extremely contagious as everyone began to secretly plan what they would do in the show. Quickly, we all signed our names on the sign-up sheet and headed for class. We were pumped and ready to jam.

For the rest of the day, William sat in class doodling and trying to come up with a name for the band. Eventually, near the end of the day he had created what he would call the greatest name ever for a band. He folded the piece of paper that had the name on it and said he would share it with us after school. We would have to wait.

It didn't take long for the bell to ring, and we were quietly dismissed for the day. The hallways rang with excitement as all the kids talked about the upcoming auditions. We got all our belongings from our lockers and headed for the bus line. After a few minutes of pleading with William to share the name of the band, both Zoey and I gave up. We'd have to wait until we got to William's.

Zoey and I both arrived at the same time to William's house and noticed a sign on the garage door. Apparently, we were to wait outside until the grand unveiling ceremony. We could hear someone moving around in the garage. It must have been

William. He was up to something. It took roughly fifteen minutes when we finally heard some music start playing in the garage. Then the garage door began to open. We entered the garage and saw William smiling and standing beside the drums. On the front of the drums was a blanket covering the bass drum. He pointed at the drum and slowly began to pull the blanket away. Zoey and I watched anticipating the name of our new band. That's when we both noticed the name: Rock Frog.

We didn't know what to say. William smiled with joy as he shouted out the name. "Rock Frog!" I was speechless. I thought it was supposed to be the greatest name ever for a band. That wasn't what I was expecting. I was a bit disappointed when Zoey finally spoke up and said, "That's Cool!" Well, if Zoey thought it was cool, then it must have been cool. And with that, the name of our band was born. From that day forward, we would be part of history.

I was curious as to how William had the name

on the front skin. I bent down to see that he had used some black hockey tape to make up the lettering. As I continued to stare at the name, it was slowly starting to come around to me. Upon further inspection, I noticed some initials on the drumkit. On the side of the bass drum were the letters N. P. I immediately showed the other two. We had no clue as to who or what they stood for. Just then William's dad came into the garage and began checking out our gear. He sat down at the drums and began twirling the drumsticks in the air just like a real rock star. Then out of nowhere, he began playing the drums like a madman. He started off slowly and built up speed. It turned out that William's dad was amazing. After about fifteen minutes of playing, his dad stopped and offered to help me out if I'd like some pointers and then headed back into the house. Just before he left, he turned and told us to look up the band **RUSH**. Then without saying anything else he disappeared as the door closed. Not in our wildest dreams had we expected that to happen. William stared towards the door for a second or two, scratched his head, and headed to the workbench. Then he called us over to see the next part of his plan.

Plan B as William called it, had an illustration of our new band up on the stage. William was rocking on lead guitar. Zoey was jamming on the bass and I was center stage hammering on the drums. It looked so cool seeing the three of us in the plan.

We were super impressed by William's plan when I noticed two things on it. The first one was neat, the second one not! Above the crowd watching us play were the words 'Greatest song EVER!!!' It was wicked! However, it was the second thing he added that I didn't like. Above my character playing the drums were the words 'terrible drummer (Thomas)'. William laughed and pointed it out. Zoey chuckled for a second and could see I was upset. She soon encouraged William to erase it and eventually he removed it from the plan. (See. I told you Zoey wasn't so bad.)

William then began to explain his newest plan. All we had to do was come up with a simple, easy song to play in the talent show. As he stated, all we had to do was use a few power chords and it'd be gold.

Surprisingly, it didn't take long to come up with a half decent song. Within hours, we had the music and lyrics completed. We rehearsed a few times and decided to call it quits for the day. We agreed to return the next day to rehearse and make any additional changes if we had to. The good news was that we had roughly a month to rehearse and prepare for the auditions.

Weeks passed and we continued to rehearse. Day by day we improved until it was time to audition. To makes things easy, Mr. Mousseau told us to make a video and bring it in. That way we wouldn't have to lug all our equipment back and forth. So, we recorded a video and brought it to school.

It was the day of the auditions and all the acts had to meet in the gym. One by one the acts performed. Finally, Miss Sims, one of our rotary teachers called us up to play our video. We marched up to the front of the gym and opened the file on my Chromebook. I let William press play. First it was Miss Sims who stood in disbelief. Then Mr. Mousseau stared as his jaw dropped to the floor. They were amazed at just how good we were. After a brief discussion they both agreed that we would end the show. We were in the show! Now we had two weeks to get ready.

Time flew and it was the day of the big show. We had already set our equipment up the night before which made it a lot easier for us. Now all we had to do was wait for the final act. One by one the kids performed from juggling acts, to stand-up comedy, dancing, and even karate demonstrations. We were moments away from the biggest performance of our lives when William told us he had a special surprise. We begged him to tell us as we were called backstage to get ready. He just kept telling us it was a surprise and that we'd have to wait.

The second last act performed and were taking a bow when the curtains closed. They hustled off as we moved our equipment right to the front of the stage. Our hearts were pumping. We could hear the crowd begin to cheer. "William! William! William!"

Mr. Mousseau then announced our name and the curtains opened. The entire audience burst into a roar. Once the crowd settled down, I counted us in, and we began to play. Everything was going great as the crowd stood on their feet. Even some of the teachers were now in the front row pumping their fists in the air. We were almost finished when we noticed Mr. Pitts, our principal, standing at the front of the stage talking photos. William kicked a foot pedal towards my drums. Then without warning he stomped on it.

Within seconds the front of my bass drum exploded off and confetti poured out into the crowd. Unfortunately, for Mr. Pitts, he was hit in the head by the flying drum skin. The crowd erupted into a frenzy as smoke poured out of my drums. Then the fire alarm sounded and just like that it was over. The entire audience had to be evacuated out the side fire exits. The big kids cheered as the smaller ones began to cry. It was pandemonium!

Eventually, things settled, and the students were allowed back into the school. During all the commotion, I had lost sight of William. On my way back to class, I could see him standing at the office talking to the principal and the fire department. I had a feeling I wasn't going to be seeing him at school for quite some time.

William was suspended for a few days for bringing pyrotechnics to school. He also had to help set up any future assemblies for the remainder of the school year. However, there was a silver lining to the whole talent show incident. One of the parents in the audience had taped the whole thing on their phone and uploaded our act to YouTube. Within days, our video went viral and the three of us became legends at school and in our community. It was so cool because now everyone knew who Rock Frog was!

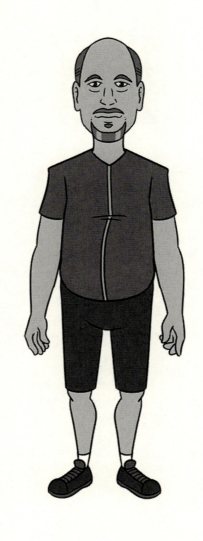

WILL MR. MOUSSEAU RETURN?

I HOPE SO!

About the Author

Mark Gunning grew up in Chippawa, Ontario where he spent most of his youth playing outside with his friends. They had many fun adventures together and this has helped create some of the stories you have enjoyed today.

A teacher with the DSBN for over twenty years, Mark started sharing some of his stories with his students. They enjoyed them so much, in 2017 he finally wrote his first book, The Adventures of William and Thomas. Today he continues to create more great stories. He and his wife Stephanie, have three children, two cats, and two dogs named Ozzie and Chewie. (Watch for them in the latest adventure of Secret Agent PurrKins!)

They'll Be Back!

Fantastic news everyone. I hear that William and Thomas will be back soon. And just when the neighbourhood thought it was safe. What do they have planned this time? No one knows for sure, but we can bet that's it going to be awesome. Will Granny Grunt return? Who knows? Will Mr. Mousseau return? Who knows? Will there be a UFO? I hope so!

Check out the website to find out more and keep up to date by signing up for the monthly newsletter. You can find a link for this at www.itchygooneybooks.com.

I Told You So!

Back 4 More

Coming Soon

AND NOW FOR ANOTHER

COMIC ADVENTURE

BY THOMAS

Secret   Agent Purrkins

in

The Stolen
Cat Toy

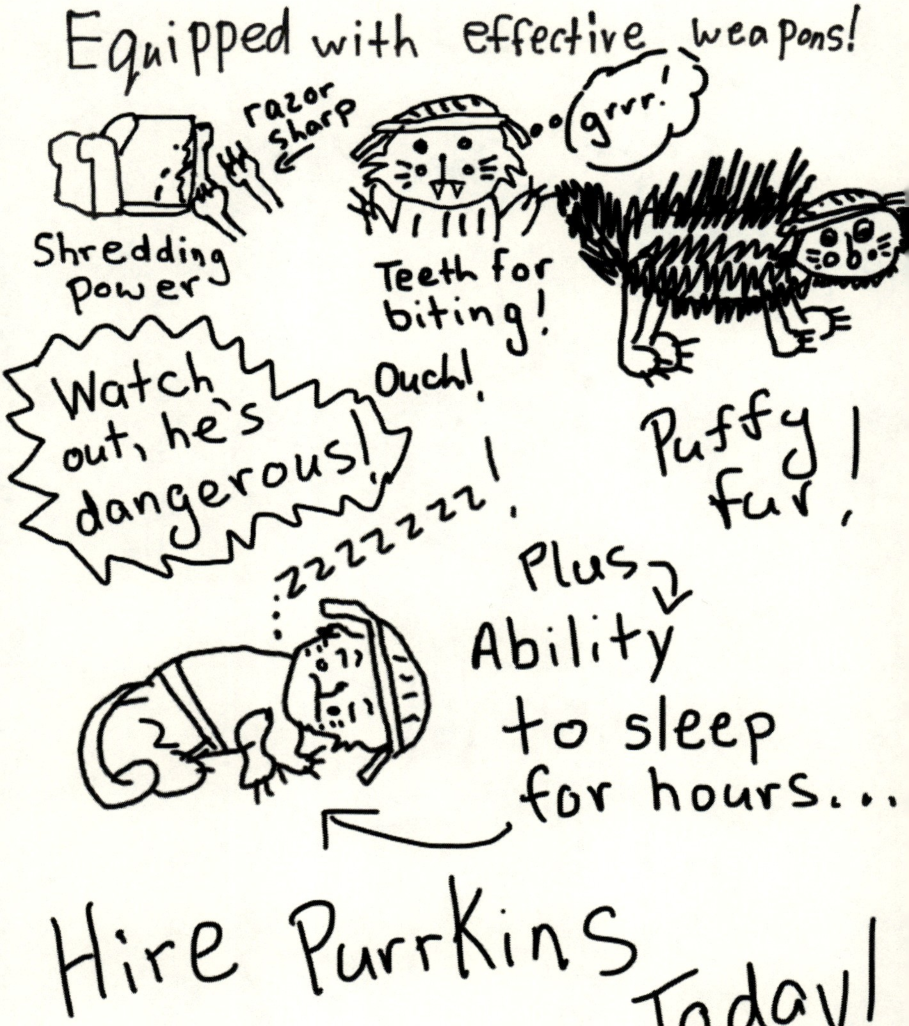
Equipped with effective weapons!
razor sharp
Shredding power
grrr!
Teeth for biting!
Watch out, he's dangerous!
Ouch!
Puffy fur!
zzzzzzzzz!
Plus Ability to sleep for hours...
Hire Purrkins Today!

Secret Agent Purrkins Episode 2

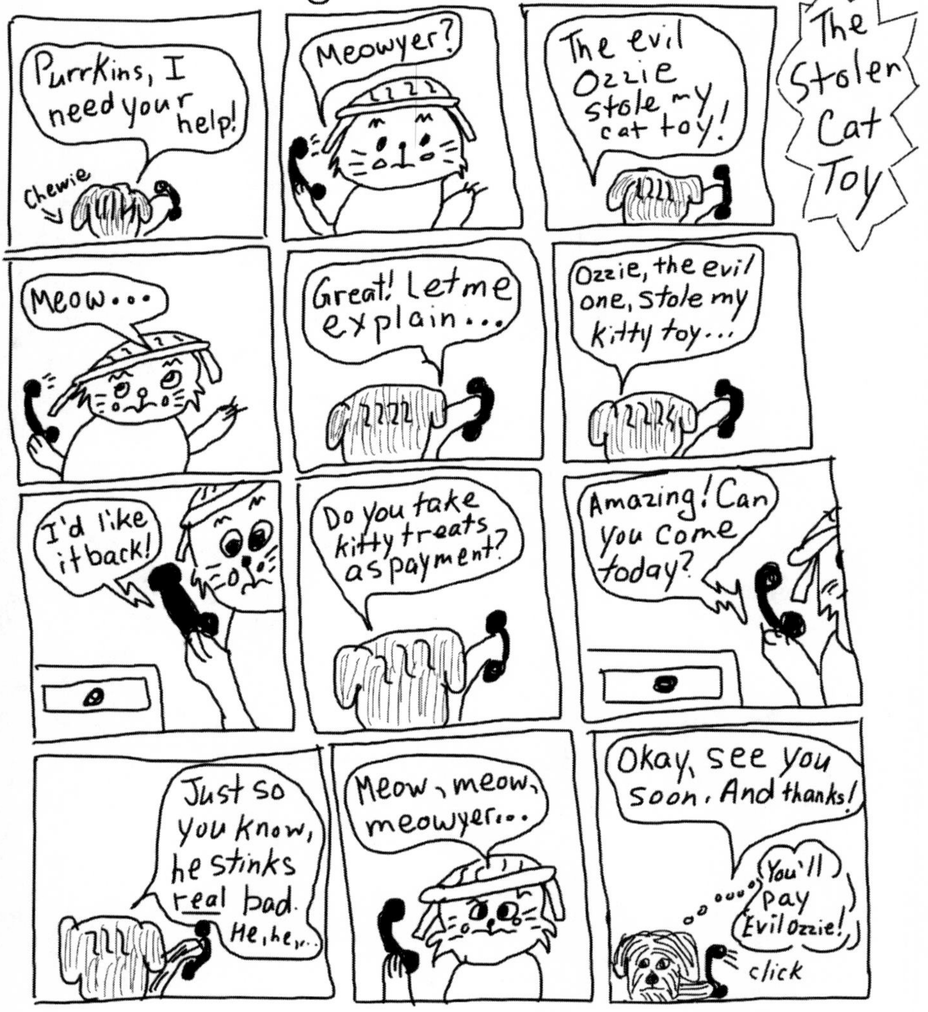

Stay tuned for more adventures with Secret Agent Purrkins!

Hey kids, do you have an idea for the next great episode of Secret Agent PurrKins? If you do, be sure to drop me a message telling me about your idea. Who knows? Why it may even end up in one of my upcoming books!

See you next time!

www.itchygooneybooks.com

www.facebook.com/itchygooneybooks/

 @MGunningAuthor

 @markgunningitys

Manufactured by Amazon.ca
Acheson, AB

13519627R00065